'The love I have for you will never fade. My
desire for you will only grow. And the life we
share together will make every day worth living.'
~Auggie~

For Nicole, Mom, Sonya, Paula and Lucii

A Marked Heart Novella

M. Sembera

C&A Novella
Copyright 2015 © M. Sembera
ISBN-13: 978-0692417614
Edited by Lucii Grubb
Cover Design Copyright 2015 © M. Sembera
Grigoriev Ruslan/Shutterstock
Published by
Broken Bird Media

Table of Contents

He was all the things she really wanted and never bothered to look for in a man. He was also the most stubborn jackass she had ever met.

She was an infuriating pain in the ass, and he'd be damned straight to hell if he had to spend even one day without her by his side.

Chapter 1

A glow of curtain muted sunlight fell across the bed as Charlotte watched Auggie lying on his back next to her asleep. He was all the things she really wanted and never bothered to look for in a man. He was also the most stubborn jackass she had ever met, but somehow that made her love him even more. She leaned closer, walking her fingers around the new tattoo his cousin Kieran had marked him with the day before, that sat on the left side of his chest.

Auggie's words from the previous night flickered in her mind.

'It's not the prettiest wrapping but what's underneath belongs to you.'
His heart belonged to her and as a permanent declaration he had marked it with a black peacock feather and keeping with a long standing Caffrey family tradition, there was a Celtic heart where the eye of the feather would be. Then he knelt and proposed.

'Charlotte Persephone Roberts, you are worth more than I will ever have to offer but if

you marry me, I swear I'll do everything possible to be worthy of you.'

A happy sigh escaped her as she thought about their now matching peacock feather tattoos. Hers was across her shoulder blade in white ink. Up until the moment she saw his fresh ink last night, the Celtic cross that covered his back, which he got when his brother William passed away, had always been her favorite of his tattoos.

Charlotte's fingers continued their steady path, circling his tattoo, when she noticed him waking up.

"Lookin' to start the day off right, Lotte?" He questioned in a low tone.

The corner of her mouth curled into a smile as she leaned over him before running her fingers through his beard while her lips brushed against the side of his neck.

~

Waiting for her waffles to pop out of the toaster, Charlotte stood in Auggie's kitchen. She felt his hands slide around her hips as he stood behind her. Placing light kisses down the side of her neck, he tugged her closer.

"No, sir." She blurted with a laugh, turning to face him as she pulled away.

Scowling at her, Auggie griped, "No?" As if she had just told him she changed her mind about being engaged.

Giving him a little reminder, Charlotte held up her left hand and wiggled the back of her princess cut peacock blue diamond engagement ring up and down with her thumb, saying, "We need to go see Emerson and Amila."

"They knew I was gonna propose." He argued pulling her against him.

Distracted when Auggie pressed his lips to hers, Charlotte jumped slightly breaking their kiss when she heard the toaster pop.

"Breakfast is ready." She quickly alerted, reminding herself this time, all that was needed to accomplish for the day.

Auggie groaned as she pulled away from him to fix their plates.

As they sat at his table eating breakfast, Charlotte rested one of her legs across Auggie's lap while the other was folded on her chair. He kept his hand on her shin, grazing his thumb against her skin. Along with toaster waffles, it was part of their breakfast routine when she stayed the night.

Finishing her last bite of waffles, she glanced over to see Auggie swirling a piece of his waffles around in the syrup on his plate with his fork.

"We need to go to my apartment so I can change before we go to the house."

With a short nod, Auggie set his fork down suggesting, "While we're there, you can look through Penny's recipe book and find something to cook me for dinner."

Instantly narrowing her eyes at him, she questioned, "Excuse me?"

Looking up from his plate at her, Auggie replied, "We're getting married."

"And?" Charlotte uttered with a nasty expression on her face.

"I wanna wife that cooks."

Pulling her leg from his lap, she hopped up from her chair, gave the bottom of her shirt a little tug and snapped, "Is that so?"

Turning in his chair, he scowled up at her questioning, "You expect me to eat frozen waffles for the rest of my life?"

"You could have scrambled eggs." She retorted.

"I don't like them. And how is it the one thing you cook is the only thing I don't eat?"

"How do you know? You've never had mine." She griped back at him.

"Are they eggs?" Auggie asked.
Without answering, Charlotte glared at him.

"Are they scrambled?"
Irritated, she rolled her eyes.

With a sarcastic tone, Auggie shared, "Unless they magically turn into somethin' else when you cook 'em, I'm not gonna like 'em."

"Well then you have two options, Augustus. Either you learn to like them or you learn to cook."

~

Watching Charlotte shoot him a 'so there' look before she walked off, he growled under his breath at her.

It wasn't that Auggie was helpless in the kitchen, he knew how to cook a few things but that wasn't the point. She was just being stubborn. It seemed as though the only reason she was refusing to learn was because he wanted her to.

Getting up from the table, he walked out of his kitchen before stepping into the hallway and turning the corner into his room.

A mischievous smile crossed her face as she stepped toward him, asking, "How about a compromise?"

"You mean a bribe?" He questioned, already knowing how her compromises worked.

Giving him an over exaggerated eye roll, Charlotte replied, "I propose that we compromise by you learning to cook and I will take care of dessert."

"If you're gonna make dessert, why can't you cook dinner too?"

With an aggravated expression she spouted, "You're ridiculous."

"Damn it, woman, you..." he started to gripe, trailing off as her hands slid up his chest and around to the back of his neck.

Charlotte looked into his eyes.

Her spark of mischief was back as she shared, "You and I are talking about two completely different kinds of desserts." Auggie's scowl was quickly replaced by a smile as she clarified, "And you can have mine before and after dinner if you like."

Nodding, he agreed to her compromise.

Chapter 2

The second Auggie and Charlotte stepped foot into her apartment, his sister Penny practically tackled them. Blurting out her congratulations as she held onto the both of them, it took a good ten minutes before they were able to get through the door.

With an excited smile Penny finally let go and took a step back, but only for a second.

"We're going to be sisters!" She cheered at Charlotte lunging at her for another hug.

As Charlotte hugged Penny back, saying, "I know, there's so much to do. You'll be my maid of honor, right?" Auggie took the opportunity to step away and escape being the next victim of Penny's over enthusiastic behavior.

"Damn, you'd think y'all were getting married." He grumbled, watching them continue to chatter their excitement while letting go and then hugging each other again and again.

It wasn't that he was jealous of his sister but there were still some hard feelings surrounding Charlotte's decision to get an apartment with Penny instead of staying with him. It wasn't that he didn't trust Charlotte either, he knew she would never give another man the time of day. It was knowing how close he came to losing her, due to his own suborn ass pride, that caused him to have an irrational need to have her close at all times.

When Penny and Charlotte were finally finished with their almost sister hug-fest, Penny quickly whipped around to face Auggie.

"Let's see it!"

Taking a step back, Auggie teased, "The rings on her finger not mine."

Placing her hand on her hip, Penny laughed, "No stupid, your mark. I wanna see it."

"Nope."

"That's not fair!" Penny blurted before saying, "It's not every day that I get to..." Seeing a curious expression spread across Charlotte's face, Auggie quickly cut his sister off.

Scowling at her, he griped, "I said no." Penny narrowed her eyes at him before turning back to Charlotte with a smile.

"Oh-kay." Charlotte uttered, giving them both a strange look and sharing, "I'm going to go get changed."
Both Auggie and Penny watched as Charlotte walked out of the living room.

The moment Auggie heard Charlotte's door close, his sister turned and glared at him.

In a hushed tone, Penny fussed, "I cannot believe you."

"Drop it, Pen." He snapped back at her walking into the kitchen.

Following close behind, she continued to fuss; "Why wouldn't you just tell her? It's not like she thinks mom likes her or anything."

Reaching on top of the refrigerator and grabbing Penny's book of family recipes, Auggie shared, "She made a point last night to ask if mom gave us her blessing."

"So you lied?"

"No." He griped before explaining, "I told her mom is the family drawer and I have her mark on my chest."

"So you lied."

"No, what I said was true. I have Charlotte's mark and mom is the drawer for our family."

Pursing her lips at him, Penny questioned, "And what are you gonna do when she finds out your truths are unrelated?"

"Unless you're gonna tell her that mom refused and you drew it out for me, she won't."

With a heavy sigh, she replied, "Fine."
After a nod of appreciation to Penny, Auggie set her recipe book on the counter and opened it up.

Flipping through the pages, he could feel his sister staring at him.

"What?"

"I'm not going to tell her but I really think you should."

With a low growl of irritation, Auggie decided to turn the tables on her.

"When were you gonna tell me you're working at Kieran's shop?"

There was a long pause before she asked, "Who said that I was?"

"Word gets around."

"Are you mad?" Penny questioned in a cautious tone.

"Nah, Kieran said his floors have never been cleaner." He teased, wondering if she would fess up and admit that she was apprenticing for him.

Glancing off to the side, Penny changed the subject.

"What are you doing with my recipe book, anyways?"

Flipping the page, Auggie replied, "Looking for something to cook for dinner."

Penny appeared confused at first then quickly burst into laughter.

Chapter 3

Walking up to her family's house, Charlotte stopped a few feet from her parent's front door. Holding her hand, Auggie turned giving her a questioning expression.

"Are you sure you're ready for this?"

Stepping closer to her, Auggie grabbed her other hand, replying, "How bad could it be?"

With a little laugh, she informed, "You have no idea." Just as the front door swung open.

"You're here!" Amila greeted before hollering back into the house, "They're here!"
Patting him on the chest, Charlotte smiled up at him before they continued into the house.

Everyone crowded around Charlotte and Auggie as they stepped inside. Amila's smile beamed at them as Emerson stepped to Auggie and shook his hand.

"Congratulations." He stated with a warm smile.

With an appreciative nod, Auggie replied, "Thank you."

"Well, let's hear it, how did you propose?" Amila eagerly questioned.

Charlotte's younger brothers, Max and Luke, said a quick congratulations before heading back upstairs while her sisters, Silvia, Jenna and Lola, waited to hear the proposal details.

Reaching over, Charlotte placed her hand in Auggie's as she shared how Auggie asked her to marry him.

"How romantic." Amila swooned before Charlotte's youngest sister Lola chimed in.

"And then what happened?"
Charlotte instantly glanced at her fiancé as she recalled how he responded to her 'kiss me,' with breathtaking urgency at the bar and again when they arrived at his house.

"Uhh..." Charlotte uttered, trying to come up with something that was appropriate for a ten year old to hear.

Amila quickly covered for her, stating, "And then, they shook hands and said goodnight."

"Really?" Lola blurted in disbelief.

Nodding, Auggie lied, "Yep kid, that's exactly what happened."

With a disappointed sigh, Lola looked directly at Auggie informing, "You really should have kissed her."

Leaning her forehead to Auggie's shoulder, Charlotte laughed at her little sister giving him advice.

The entire coffee table was covered in bridal magazines almost a foot high and sitting right on top of them was a large white binder.

As the girls sat down to start making wedding plans, Auggie asked, "How many weddings are we having?"

All five of them looked at him like he had just committed a sin as Emerson patted Auggie on the back with a laugh offering, "Why don't you and I step out back and leave the ladies to their planning."

Charlotte gave Auggie a soft smile before watching him walk out of the living room with Emerson.

Admitting to herself, even she was overwhelmed by the amount of preparation suddenly expected of her.

Charlotte turned to Amila, saying, "He just proposed, we haven't set a date."

Amila gave an understanding smile as she replied, "I guess I'm over doing it a tad. I'm just so excited, honey."

Reaching an arm around Amila, Charlotte hugged her.

"Who is your maid of honor?" Silvia interrupted.

"Penny." Charlotte replied as she pulled away from Amila.

"Are you kidding?"

Shaking her head at her sister, Charlotte stated, "No, I'm not."

Glaring at Charlotte, Silvia whined, "You're going to ruin the whole day."

"Seriously?"

Hopping up, Silvia shouted, "Not everything is always about you all the time!" As she stomped up the stairs.

Turning to Amila again, Charlotte questioned, "Seriously?"

Before Amila could answer, Jenna spoke up sharing, "She wants to walk down the aisle with Braden."

As Lola giggled, Charlotte let out a frustrated sigh and shook her head.

~

Leaning up against the side of the garage, Auggie watched Emerson as he appeared to be thinking of something to say.

"So this is gonna be a big thing?"

Emerson smiled assuring, "I am sure it will be."

Running his hand down the front of his beard, Auggie asked, "What do I need to do?"

"Stay out of the way. Weddings are for the bride no matter what anyone else tells you. All you need to do is go along with everything she says and tell her everything she picks is perfect."

"What?"

With an amused expression, Emerson questioned, "Do you want to survive the wedding?"

"Yeah."

"Then take my advice."

Auggie griped, "Perfect," before Emerson stated, "That's the spirit. Now, let's head back in." Pushing away from the wall, Auggie thought, 'Great,' as he followed Emerson back inside.

Chapter 4

Charlotte sat with her arms crossed in the passenger seat of Auggie's truck as he drove them to Ren and Jackson's house. After ten minutes of complaining about her sister being a brat, she immediately started griping at Auggie when he said there was no need to make a stop at his mom's house.

In Auggie's mind, she was already irritated and making a bigger deal out of it then necessary.

"You can't be mad about this?"

Whipping her head around, Charlotte snapped, "Now you're telling me what to do?"
With a loud groan Auggie gripped the steering wheel tighter.

"It was a question."

"It didn't sound like a question." Charlotte bit back at him.

Thinking two can play at this game, he agreed; "Fine, it wasn't a question."

"Oh, so you are telling me what to do."

Waiting for the snap, Auggie nodded, adding, "Damn right."

Pulling onto his cousin Jackson's property, he stopped his truck right outside the gate and turned to look at Charlotte.

Her eyes were wild and her face was flush. It was a beautiful sight, one that instantly caused his muscles to tense and his heart to pound in his chest. Whether he was bringing her to the point of unbridled anger or ecstasy, it held all the passion that she loved him with.

Shifting his truck into park, he scowled at her.

"You listen here, Augustus Caffrey. Putting a ring on my finger doesn't give you any authority over me."

"Is that right?" He questioned, finding it a bit hard not to smile at her at this point.

Narrowing her eyes at him, she continued, "That's exactly right and don't you even think for a second that it does."

"Ya done?"

"Not even close."

Reaching for his door handle, Auggie teased, "Well, could you put your little fit on pause for minute so we can go get congratulated."

"Are your serious right now?"

Growing frustrated with her, Auggie sighed; "Are you?"

Just as she was about to start shouting, he opened his door and jumped out, slamming it closed before she had the chance.

Stomping to the gate, Auggie growled under his breath at her. He pulled the pin to unlatch the gate before walking it open. This woman was going to give him hell for the rest of their lives together. As he walked back to his truck, he could only shake his head at himself. She was an infuriating pain in the ass, and he'd be damned straight to hell if he had to spend even one day without her by his side.

After climbing back into his truck and pulling up past the gate, Auggie stopped the truck again and turned it off.

"You comin' in?" He asked noticing she still had her seat belt on.

Without looking at him, Charlotte questioned, "Is there something you wanna tell me?"

"There's a hell of a lot of things I'd like to tell you right now." He fussed at her.

"Do any of them include the real reason we're not going to your mom's?"

Auggie stared at her, quickly realizing this was serious.

He knew he should have told her the truth to begin with but he didn't so now he was stuck trying to cover his own ass, hoping she didn't find out.

"Why are you all of the sudden wanting to visit her? You don't even like her."

Appearing offended, Charlotte replied, "I don't dislike her."

"Okay, let's just pretend that's true." He started before she cut him off saying, "It is and I honestly don't care how she feels about me."

"Then what's the real reason you're mad?" He sarcastically asked.

"Because I do care how she feels about you." Now Auggie just felt like crap.

"You have a close family and I don't want to be someone that comes between y'all."

"Look, Lotte, everyone's had their turn at being on mom's bad side. This just happens to be mine."

A soft smile formed as she replied, "You swear she'll get over it and be at the wedding?"

"I sure do and ya know I'd be nice next time if you would just say what's on your mind instead of doing that woman thing you do."
In an instant, her smile was gone.

"Excuse me?"

"What?"

Angry all over again, Charlotte popped the button on her seatbelt and flung it off her as she swung the door open snapping, "You're ridiculous." While climbing out of his truck.
Auggie gave a loud sigh and opened his door as hers slammed shut.

Catching up with her at the front door, Auggie wanted to calm her down before they went in. He didn't mind her being mad at him, she'd get over it like always, but he knew Ren would instantly take her side and then he'd have two crazy women ticked off at him.

Just as he was about to try and make things right, the door opened and Ren chirped, "I can't believe ya'll are getting married."

"I can't believe what a damn jackass he is." Charlotte replied as she stepped in.

Ren looked up at Auggie with a disapproving glare before turning and walking with Charlotte into the living room.

With a wide smile, Jackson patted him on the back laughing, "Congrats, and good luck. This is only the first day."

Shaking his head, Auggie couldn't help but let out a laugh of his own as he reached over and shook Jackson's hand.

Chapter 5

Once Liv texted back that the movie she and Kieran were at was almost over, and that Charlotte and Auggie could let themselves in to wait for them, Charlotte followed Auggie into their house.

Making herself comfortable on the couch, Charlotte was glad this was their last stop. Even though Auggie had been an ass most of the day, she looked forward to going back to his house.

As Auggie sat down next to her, Charlotte asked, "Did you have a specific date in mind?"

"For what?"

Rolling her eyes at him, she replied, "Our wedding."

The side of his faced scrunched up into a smile as he replied, "I'm ready whenever you are."

"Amila said The Society is involving themselves."

Leaning closer, he teased, "I knew getting roped up with you was a bad idea."

The corner of her mouth curled into a smile as she agreed, "Worst idea ever."

"Nope, the worst is you agreeing to marry me."

Letting out a little laugh, Charlotte asked, "Is that so?"

"You're stuck with me now."

"That's where you're wrong." She assured before inching closer as she shared, "You, sir, are stuck with me."

"Ah, hell." Auggie griped, before smiling at her again and giving her a quick kiss.

The moment he did, Liv and Kieran walked in.

Charlotte and Auggie both stood to greet them as they strolled into the house.

Reaching out his hand to Auggie, Kieran laughed, "Never thought you'd actually do it."

Charlotte shook her head at them as Auggie replied, "What can I say, she got me."

Liv clapped her hands together taunting, "Ha! I never thought she'd say yes." Before patting him on the shoulder saying, "Congrats Auggs." As she winked at Charlotte.

A whole new level of excitement filled Charlotte as she realized, now that everyone had been notified in person, it was official. They were getting married.

As Charlotte and Liv stepped away from Auggie and Kieran, she decided the wedding wouldn't be complete without Liv being a part of it.

"So, Penny's going to be my maid of honor. Will you be one of my bridesmaids?"

Liv quickly let out a laugh before declining, "Nah, I don't do that."

Charlotte was about to ask her what she meant but was side tracked when she heard Auggie say, "Best man?"

When Kieran accepted by saying, "For sure," Charlotte turned and questioned, "Kieran's your best man?"

"Yeah, who else would it be?"

Charlotte glanced at Liv who appeared just as surprised before the both blurted, "Braden," in unison.

"Pretty sure best man requires a man." Kieran laughed, earning a hard glare from Liv.

Auggie smiled at his cousin's remark before informing, "It's Kieran."

Even though Charlotte felt he was wrong for picking his cousin over his brother, she really couldn't argue since she picked Penny over her own sister.

Auggie and Kieran made their way outside to the porch, closing the door behind themselves.

As soon as the door shut, Liv shook her head mumbling, "Stupid ass."

Following her to the kitchen, Charlotte asked, "Are ya'll any better?"

"Hell no." Liv snapped before sliding onto a barstool beside her island, sharing, "I get that it's a big deal. He feels bad for marking Braden but it shouldn't be affecting us."

"Us as in..."

Shaking her head Liv answered, "It's like he's just going through the motions, ya know."
Nodding, Charlotte stayed silent.

Quickly changing her disposition, Liv laughed, "You and Auggs are for real, huh."

"As real as it can get." Charlotte replied with a smile.

"That's cool. You're good for him. Even though, it doesn't make a whole lotta sense."

"What do you mean?"

With a smirk on her face Liv replied, "It's Auggie. I just don't get it."

"He's the best thing that ever happened to me."

"You musta had one hell of a rough start for that to be true."

Drawing in a deep breath, Charlotte nodded before sharing, "There's a lot more to him than a scruffy beard and plaid shirt."

"If you say so."
They both started to laugh as Auggie and Kieran stepped back into the house.

Chapter 6

Running up Charlotte's apartment steps, Auggie was amazed at how fast Charlotte was able to move in those heels of hers. The session at the photography studio, to have their engagement photo in The Society Newsletter, turned out to be one of the most miserable experiences of his life. Not only did he have to wear a damn suit and tie and smile for an hour and a half but Charlotte kept whispering things in his ear. Things that made it hard for him to concentrate on what they were doing and crave the moment they were finally alone.

Now, it was time for her to make good on all those dirty little remarks she kept taunting him with.

"You know how hard that was?" He questioned in a low tone as he closed the door behind himself.

In a sleek black dress and her black stiletto heels that drove him crazy, she wore a wicked grin as she slowly walked backwards into the kitchen.

With a curious tone she teased, "Was?"

Following her, he stepped out of his dress shoes and unfastened his slacks, leaving them and his boxers behind along with his jacket and tie.

"You're fixin' to find out." He swore, unbuttoning the first two buttons of his dress shirt before pulling it over his head and tossing it on the table.

Wrapping his arms around her, Auggie backed her up against the side of the kitchen table.

Auggie's hands slid down her sides before grasping at her hips as he kissed her deeply.

"Turn around." He whispered needing to touch her skin that her dress was covering.

His hands never left her as she turned her back to him.

Slowly unzipping her dress, he pulled it down her body until it fell to the floor mumbling, "Damn," when he noticed she wasn't wearing any panties.

Slightly leaning forward, Charlotte placed her hands against the table breathing, "I want you, now."

Taking a moment to appreciate the sight of his beautiful fiancé in nothing but her heels, bent over the table in front of him, he wrapped his hands around her hips and pulled her to him.

With Charlotte's appreciation echoing through the kitchen as Auggie met her demand, the sound of the apartment door opening didn't register in his mind until he heard his sister's voice.

"What the hell!"

Swiftly pushing away from Charlotte and pulling her behind him, he saw Penny with her hands over her eyes quickly leaving the doorway.

Auggie grabbed a placemat off of the table to cover himself as Liv blurted, "Damn Auggs,"and Penny shouted from the other room, "Shut up, Liv!"

Eyeing him, Liv shared, "Ah, now I get it." Before catching on to his get the hell out glare and excusing herself saying, "I'll just go make sure Penny's not going to harm herself."

As what had just happened started to sink in, Auggie felt Charlotte shaking behind him.

Turning to her, he wrapped his arms around her, holding her tight.

"Did they see everything?"

Kissing the side of her head, he quietly replied, "No."

Shaking her head into his chest Charlotte questioned, "Are you sure?"

Reaching for his shirt, Auggie let go of her just long enough to slide his dress shirt over her head and button the top two buttons.

Taking her face in his hands, he forced her to look him in the eyes as he shared, "Liv got an eye full of me but that's all she saw. I promise."

Charlotte nodded with her eyes full of worry before stepping away from him so he could retrieve his slacks from the living room floor.

Auggie knew Charlotte would never believe her entire body was beautiful no matter how many times he told her. It had taken months for her to let him touch her all over without tensing up or flinching. Her scars were brutal but at the same time they were beautiful to him because they were a part of her. Truthfully, he was just as concerned about her being exposed, not because of her scars, because seeing all of her was a privilege in his mind and her incredible beauty was for only him to see.

Once Liv assured both Charlotte and Auggie were decent, Penny stepped into the kitchen.

Noticeably avoiding eye contact with them, Penny held up her hand announcing, "The two of you have violated the sanctity of my kitchen."

Liv started to laugh at her outlandish display then quickly admitted, "Sorry," when Penny glared at her.

"Here is what's going to happen," Penny continued before pointing to the table stating, "I want that abomination destroyed."

Clinching his back teeth together, it was getting hard for Auggie not to start laughing.

"And we are never going to speak of this horrific day again."

"Penny, I..." Charlotte started to say before Penny cut her of blurting, "Never ever!"

Chapter 7

Charlotte was relieved that it only took a few weeks with no eye contact for Penny to recover from the kitchen situation. It made talking to her so much easier.

Marking off a few more items from her bridal to do list, Charlotte was more than happy The Society had involved themselves in her event. It was such a relief to have them handling everything, just picking out what was needed was overwhelming enough.

"So what's left?"

Charlotte let out a loud huff as she replied, "I still have to pick a bouquet, place settings, linens, flowers, the wedding song, playlist for the reception, special order Auggie's vest and tie for his tux, and my dress."

Frowning at her, Penny questioned, "Why isn't my brother helping?"

"Every time I mention anything wedding related he either changes the subject or says 'that sounds perfect'."

"You should tell him he needs to get with the program."

Pausing for a moment, Charlotte hesitantly asked, "Why do you think he wants to get married?"

"Umm, because he's in love with you." Penny laughed.

"I know he is but do you think he's marrying me because I won't live with him or because he wants to be married."

With a curious expression, Penny replied, "Neither, I think Auggie is marrying you because he wants you to be his wife."

"Can I be honest with you?"

"Always." Penny swore with a serious expression.
Charlotte glanced away deciding if she really wanted to confide in Penny.

"I'm not so sure I'll be a good wife."

A compassionate expression formed as Penny asked, "Why would you say that?"

"I can't give him kids."

"So?"

"What if he wants them?"

"Does he?"

Charlotte admitted, "He hasn't said but what if it's because he knows I can't."

"So ask him." Penny all but demanded.

"I don't want the answer."

Hopping off of Charlotte's bed, Penny warned, "We both know ignorance isn't bliss."
Nodding, Charlotte watched her walk out of the room.

~

Sitting behind her desk at The Dog House, Charlotte appreciated Penny's advice, knowing it came from her heart, but felt like Liv might be the better one to talk to.

Picking her cell phone up off of the corner of her desk, Charlotte sent Liv a text.

C: Hey, you up?

It only took a minute for Liv to text back.

L: Yep. Reading.

C: Oh, what are you reading?

L: Porn

Letting out a laugh, she texted back.

C: O.O

L: 5 ways to fix a marriage.

C: And one of them includes porn?

L: Ha! Nah, I'm reading 5 ways to fix a marriage.

C: It's that bad?

L: It's not getting any better.

Taking a deep breath, Charlotte decided not to bother Liv with her problem since she had enough to deal with in her own relationship.

C: Sorry...

L: Eh, it is what it is. Did you need somethin'?

C: Just wanted to say hi.

L: Hi! Catch ya later ;)

C: Bye :)

With a loud huff, Charlotte set her phone back on her desk and leaned back in her chair.

Not long after texting with Liv, Auggie walked in her office.

"You comin' home with me tonight?" he asked with an in inviting smile.

Closing out her computer screen, Charlotte replied, "I better go home so I can keep an eye on Penny."

Scowling he griped, "What for?"

"She's stalking the neighbor."

"What?"

Nodding at him she replied, "With muffins."

Laughing, Auggie shook his head saying, "Well, alright."

Charlotte laughed with him for a moment before standing up and walking around to the front of her desk.

Tilting her head to the side she flashed a mischievous grin.

"But, we can always say goodnight here before we go."

"Right here?" He questioned, stepping closer to her.

Sliding her hands up his chest and around to the back of his neck, Charlotte asked, "Are you all closed up?"

Auggie nodded as his hands circled her hips.

Chapter 8

What started out as an amazing day of finding the perfect wedding dress, progressed into disappointment and then irritation before ending in an all-out mess for everyone.

Initially, Charlotte had been upset with Liv for bailing on her at the bridal shop. Then, when she showed up at The Dog House, for no other reason than to drink her marital problems away, Charlotte felt bad for being selfish.

She was excited to see Penny's stalking had finally paid off enough for Seth to show up with her and even though Auggie couldn't keep his big mouth shut they seemed to be getting along fine. That was until Brooks walked over to them. Then, everything went bad.

Seth left and Braden's ex Lily showed up. If it had been up to Charlotte, both Lily and Brooks would have been limping out of the bar for hurting Penny but instead, they both walked out unharmed after the trouble they caused, leaving Braden more broken than he already was.

The worst part was, after all that, Kieran showed up right when Liv has yelling at Braden for letting Lily, once again, get the better of him. Charlotte could see how badly everyone was hurt but for some reason her soon to be husband didn't seem to care.

Not long after Liv left with Penny, Kieran spent a minute privately talking to Auggie and then left also. Auggie walked straight through the double doors to the back, more agitated than sympathetic.

"Some friend you got there." Charlotte heard Auggie shout from the office in the back.

"Who are you tellin'?" Braden snapped back as she walked in on them.

Giving him a little shove, Auggie griped, "You should have put a stop to him dating Penny in the first place."

Quickly shoving back, Braden spouted, "Don't put this on me. Brooks cheated with Lily. I'm not responsible for that."

"The hell you aren't. You brought all..." Auggie growled before Charlotte couldn't take it anymore and stepped in.

"This is not his fault."

With a deep scowl on his face, Auggie turned and glared at her.

"Are you okay?" She asked Braden in a sympathetic tone.

Pushing past his brother, Braden spit out, "Nah, I'm pretty far from okay, but thanks for askin', Charlotte," as he left.

Shaking her head, Charlotte was furious.

Walking behind the desk to grab her purse, she couldn't believe what an ass Auggie was being.

Shooting him a dirty look when, he griped, "What?" at her, Charlotte fussed, "Why can't you just tell him you're worried about him and sad that he's giving up, instead of yelling and blaming him for what we both know is hurting him too."

"Braden needs to grow up. He wears his heart on his sleeve like a damn badge of honor and you see where that's gotten him. His dumbass caused all of this right down to guilting Kieran into marking him. He's too old to only be thinking about himself, he needs to stop playing around and be a man."

Narrowing her eyes at him, she snapped, "Oh, like Kieran? Who hides behind his legacy and treats his wife like she's done something when he's the one with the problem."

"That's between them."

Shocked, Charlotte shouted, "Seriously? You stay on Braden's ass about everything but you can't bring yourself to say, 'hey, Kieran, maybe you should quit being a dick to your wife?'"

"Kieran's not my brother!" Auggie barked at her before assuring, "Braden is and he needs more guidance than beer and pizza with his buddy Liv."

"That's right! So why don't you try being his brother! You're not his dad!"

Noticeably taken aback by her words, Auggie replied, "I know that."

"Is this how he would want you to 'guide' your brother?"

Auggie's jaw clinched as he scowled and looked away replying, "I don't know 'cause I'm not him and he's not here."
Charlotte started to place her hand on his arm, knowing she had hit a sore subject with him. Instead of accepting her comfort, he turned and walked out of the room.

Auggie's dad Gus was many different things, depending who you talked to. According to Emerson, Gus was a thoughtful bartender when his life was in shambles. Ren always swore that Gus was one of the best men she had ever known. Penny adored her dad and often mentioned how loving and supportive he was. Braden never said too much unless they were joking around but made it a point several times to say he was always at the bar. Gus and Kieran's dad were close, she imagined the same way Auggie and Kieran were and any mention of Gus was always started with the fact that he was cool as hell. But since getting to know all of them, Charlotte knew, Gus was more than the man he was named after, funny stories, and poignant advice, to Auggie, his dad was everything.

Stepping out of the office, Charlotte saw Auggie standing by the back door waiting for her.

When she made it to his side, Auggie turned to her and confessed, "Braden is great at everything he does. He has the potential to be or do whatever he wants and I'm afraid he's going to waste his life being a spectacular dumbass."
Nodding, Charlotte wrapped her arms around his waist and kissed his cheek.

Chapter 9

Kissing Auggie as she buttoned the front of his shirt for him, Charlotte couldn't imagine how hard Liv's situation was. There was a certain amount of extra fulfillment knowing the man she was in love with wanted her every minute of every day. If one day he suddenly stopped, there was no doubt in her mind she wouldn't take it half as well as Liv was. As she slid his beanie over his head, Charlotte kissed him once more before they walked out to his truck.

On the way to her apartment, Charlotte mentally went over her checklist hoping to get as much done as possible today.

"Do you want to look through linen patterns with me?"

Without giving it a thought, he replied, "I'm sure whatever you pick will be perfect."

Rolling her eyes as she stared out of the window, Charlotte thought about all the articles she had read in bridal magazines. Finding it a little pathetic that was where she had resorted to drawing advice from, she started to laugh.

"Somethin' funny?"

Smiling at him she replied, "In one of the magazines I have, there was an article on abstaining from sex for at least two weeks before the wedding."

Watching him scowl and glance at her from the corner of his eye, she couldn't resist messing with him.

"We should do that." She teased trying to keep a straight face.

"Nope."

Cracking a smile she asked, "No?"

"Not no. Hell no!"

Put off by his tone, Charlotte snapped, "No?"

"You must be high outta your mind if you think I'm agreein' to that."

As they pulled into the apartment complex parking lot, she acknowledged the fact that she didn't want to abstain either but the fact that he flat out was telling her no, forced her hand.

Narrowing her eyes at him she informed, "I actually don't need you to agree, Augustus."

She didn't wait for him to respond before flinging the passenger door open, hopping out of his truck and slamming the door behind her.

Storming into her apartment, she forced a quick smile at Penny but all she could think about was how he hadn't done a single thing to help with the wedding and now he was telling her no.

"Stop following me!" She griped, when she saw Auggie walk in.

"Quit tryin' to run things!"

Offended that was what he thought was going on she snapped, "It was just a suggestion."

Penny rolled her eyes and walked to the door just as he swore, "It was a stupid ass one."

With his sister now out on the balcony with the door closed behind her, Charlotte started shouting.

"That's right! I'm making decisions because you're stupid ass hasn't done one damn thing to..." she spouted before stopping suddenly when Auggie walked over and flung the door back open.

Following Auggie to see who he was talking to when she heard him growl, "You!" She saw poor Seth standing there like a deer caught in headlights as Auggie demanded, "Should the woman get to make all the decisions?"

Seth's voice was shaky as he replied, "No. I thi..."

Without letting him finish, Auggie turned back to her shouting, "Ha!"

Charlotte gave him a sarcastic smile saying, "Alright, forget about what I suggested." His expression started to soften until she narrowed her eyes informing, "It starts now," and slammed the door in his face.

~

With a loud frustrated exhale, Auggie glanced at Seth.

"Let's go." He growled, heading down the stairs.

'Who the hell did she think she was,' he thought, looking up and noticing Seth was still on the balcony.

"You comin' or what?" Auggie shouted from the bottom of the stairs.
When Seth started down the stairs, Auggie continued to his truck.

Stewing over how Charlotte was going to be the death of him the whole way out to Kieran's, he felt comfortable inviting Seth along. It was out of Auggie's character to bring outsiders in but Seth seemed like a good guy and since that made him not Penny's type, he thought it was a good show of male solidarity for him to tag along.

Kieran and Liv were sitting on the porch swing when Auggie walked up to the house with Seth right behind him.

The second he stepped foot on the porch, Liv jumped up and snapped, "Jackass," at him and marched into the house.

Without getting up, Kieran laughed, "What'd ya do?"

Reaching down and shaking Kieran's hand he swore, "Stood my ground," before sitting down on a chair next to the swing.

With a wide smile, Kieran shook his head before acknowledging Seth as he offered, "Pull up a chair, man."

While Seth appeared to be choosing just the right chair to sit in, Auggie looked at his cousin assuring, "I need a damn drink."

Chapter 10

A simple fitting for Charlotte's bridesmaids' dresses turned into an awkward yet unforgettable situation, thanks to her sister Silvia.

While they gathered in the back dressing room of Bitsie's Bridal, Charlotte's sister Silvia stared at herself in the mirror inspecting the purple satin dress she was wearing.

"Do you think he'll like it?" Silvia whispered to Jenna.

With a questioning expression, Charlotte asked, "Who? Are you bringing a date?"

Jenna quickly handed Charlotte her blue dress saying, "It fit," before making her way to the bench in the corner and burring her face in her book.

Suspicious, Charlotte asked, "What's going on?"

"Nothing." Silvia replied with a sly smile.
Charlotte glanced at Penny as she took a step back from them with a curious expression of her own.

"Silvia," Charlotte stated in a firm tone.

As if it was just a matter of time before she couldn't stand it anymore, Silvia shared, "Okay, I've decided. I'm going to seduce him."

"What?"

Looking at Charlotte as if she was the juvenile one, she continued informing, "I have it all planned out and I'm sure it will work."

"What?" Charlotte repeated, looking back at Penny who just shrugged her shoulder's with an 'oh my' expression on her face.

With a heavy sigh Silvia explained, "Weddings are the perfect setting for romance."

"Oh-kay..."

With an 'I know what I'm doing' air about her Silvia proceeded to say, "Braden wants me. I can tell. And after we walk down the aisle together..."

Charlotte instantly cut her off insisting, "No! No he does not!"

"Yes he does."

Penny's face started to match the green of her dress when she realized who Silvia was talking about.

"My brother Braden?" She clarified with a nauseated expression.

Nodding at Penny with an excited smile she replied, "Oh and don't worry, it's okay. I'm eighteen now."

"That doesn't make it okay." Charlotte stressed.

Making a 'whatever' face at Charlotte, Silvia turned to Penny saying, "Oh my gosh, Penny, Braden is like so... Mmm. He's like so incredibly hot!"

"It's bad enough he's staying with us, I don't need to hear this." Penny fussed, looking back at Charlotte.

Silvia's eyes lit up as she questioned, "He is?" Penny just stared at her with an expression that fell somewhere between disbelief and exasperation.

Thankfully, Amila walked in before the conversation could go any further.

"How's it going?"

Silvia instantly replied, "Great!" before informing, "I'm going to stay at Charlotte's tonight."

"No you're not." Charlotte snapped, wondering if her sister had lost her mind.

Confused, Amila asked, "Why not?"

Not wanting to rat her sister out, Charlotte simply stated, "She's just not."

Silvia shot a nasty look at her sister before eyeing Penny as she pleaded, "Please?"
Penny shook her head in disbelief.

"Ugh... Fine!" Silvia pouted before storming away.

"I guess she's wearing her dress home, then." Amila laughed watching her daughter make her way through the bridal shop and out of the front door.

Hanging Jenna's dress up, Charlotte griped, "Gah, that girl is something else."

Walking toward them from the corner of the room, Jenna took her dress from Charlotte and glanced at her mom commenting, "Braden."

"Oh well, she's young and Braden is handsome. All the Caffrey boys are. After all, Gus had that rough, sexy..."

Scowling at Charlotte, Penny exclaimed, "What is wrong with your family?" As she walked away.

"What did I say?"
There was nothing left for Charlotte to do, except laugh as she gave Amila a hug.

Chapter 11

After shutting down Braden's idea of having the bachelor party at a strip club, almost choking Seth out for mentioning wanting to do his little sister, and several beers, Auggie sat in a chair on Kieran's porch. No amount of alcohol could replace what he needed or alleviate the misery Charlotte's ban on sex was causing him.

By the time Charlotte arrived with Penny and Liv, it was late in the evening. He was tired and it was hard to focus on anything but Charlotte standing behind him with her arms draped over his shoulders.

Adjusting in his chair, to look back at her, Auggie asked, "Are you staying with me tonight?"

"If you can handle it." She replied in a soft tone.

Leaning his forehead to her cheek, he assured, "I wanna handle you."

He felt a smile form on her face against his forehead before she pulled back and whispered in his ear.

"Only thirteen more days."

Charlotte's words offered no relief. In that moment, they made things worse. He felt like she was being cruel. Dangling herself in front of him with her almost there but not quite assurance, Auggie was sure she was punishing him.

~

Charlotte walked into Auggie's bedroom wearing the Dog House t-shirt he gave her almost a year ago and a pair of his plaid pajama bottoms.

"Oh, what the hell?" He griped, shaking his head at her.

"What?"

Focusing on the drawstring hanging down the front of her legs, like the bow on top of a gift just waiting to be unwrapped, he barked, "Are to trying to give me a damn stroke?"

"I was trying to make it easier on you." She fussed back, irritated but clearly confused.

"Wearing somethin' of mine sure as hell isn't the way to do it."

There was no response from her this time as she stood there staring at him.

Whatever painful side effects waiting until their wedding day had caused, almost seemed pleasant at the moment. He was in agony. This wasn't a battle of wills because he had no willpower when it came to her. You can't give a man a taste of heaven and expect him to be satisfied walking the earth.

Lack of willpower aside, he wasn't willing to go one more minute playing along with her ridiculous mandate.

Pulling her against him so she could feel the proof of his words, Auggie swore, "I need you..."

He watched her pull her lips into her mouth before insisting, "You want sex."

"Ya damn right, I do." He exclaimed, without realizing how harsh he sounded, until Charlotte started to pull away.

"Wait." He pleaded before sharing, "It's more than that."

In her eyes he saw her resistance, although she allowed him to keep his arms wrapped tightly around her.

Out of desperation, he shared, "Everything is empty without you. My bed, this house, me... I need you."

Her expression changed to sympathy as she sighed and lightly kissed him.

"Remember Sophia's baby shower."

Auggie scowled as the recollection of locking himself in the back office of the bar in order to drink himself into oblivion for wanting to be with her filled his mind.

With a pained expression, he swore, "Lotte, I'm never gonna let..." Trailing off as she placed her hands on the sides of his face.

"I'm not talking about that. I want our wedding night to be special."

Scowling at her, he nodded.

Punishment wasn't what this was, it was penance. Penance for letting his stubborn as pride ruin the night she had planned for their first time together, and the next night that he had planned as well. When seeing her was still a secret and he had no idea how to handle feeling the way he did about her. He almost lost her forever and she forgave him.

However, the whole sex veto started in the first place didn't matter anymore. If special is what she wanted, that's what he would give her. He owed her that at least.

Chapter 12

There is nothing quite like attending a Society function to make getting drilled with a needle the highlight of the day.

Even though Penny agreed, set up and had the tattoo gun in her hand, she still wasn't tattooing her.

"You can do it. It's just three little lines." Charlotte encouraged as she lay fully reclined in the chair with her skirt off and one side of her panty's pulled down her thigh.

"I'm very uncomfortable with..." Penny started before Charlotte cut her off saying, "No you're not."

Frowning at her, Penny replied, "What if I mess up? These things are permanent you know."

Counting back from ten in her head, she took a deep breath and replied, "I wouldn't have asked you to do this if I didn't believe in you."
Penny took a slow deep breath of her own and nodded.

The area on the inside of Charlotte hip was sensitive and the second the needle broke her skin she winced, drawing air in through her teeth.

Suddenly, Penny sat straight up blurting, "Oh my gah! Did I hurt you?"

"Really? Penny!" Charlotte snapped out of frustration.

With an embarrassed expression she apologized, "I know. Okay. Sorry. Sorry. I'll keep going."

Closing her eyes, Charlotte leaned her head back and tried to relax and once Penny actually got started, it didn't take long at all to finish.

Charlotte hugged Penny out of appreciation before helping her close up Kieran's shop.

"How are you and Seth?"

Penny's face lit up as she replied, "Amazing."

"Is he taking you to the hospital benefit?"

With an excited nod, she questioned, "Are you going?"

"Ah...no. Your brother would never forgive me for dragging him to one of those things and honestly, my bridal shower they hosted today was enough to remind me why I gave up my chair."

"Oh." Penny pouted as she looked down at the floor.

"But... If you want, I can give you some pointers."

Nodding enthusiastically, Penny started to say something and then appeared to change her mind.

There was a slight scowl to her expression as she looked at Charlotte.

"Did you ever talk to Auggie about having kids?"

Shaking her head, Charlotte had been so busy, she honestly forgot all about that particular concern.

"I think it's better if I don't. If he's not thinking about it, I would rather not put the idea in his head."

"Aren't you curious?" Penny questioned before sharing, "It seems like that would be important to know."

Shaking her head, Charlotte replied, "Concerned is more like it."

"But he's crazy about you."

Charlotte couldn't help smiling, knowing he was, before letting a serious expression take over.

Sure he was head over heels now, but after a few years, who knew what would happen.

"Auggie said Liv and Kieran had one of those love at first sight things, but look at them."

Charlotte noticed Penny glance off to the side before saying, "Their problem isn't new. It started a long time ago, just lately, it's gotten worse."

Narrowing her eyes at Penny, Charlotte blurted, "You know what's going on with him, don't you."

Purposely avoiding eye contact, she replied, "Sorta."

"Is it really all over a stupid tattoo?"

Shaking her head, Penny appeared sad as she replied, "No, it's over a mark."
Knowing what a big deal that was to them, Charlotte dropped the subject.

Focusing on a happier relationship, she smiled at Penny.

"So, exactly how awesome is Seth?"

With a slight grimace, Penny replied, "He was fixing to show me the other morning and my mom showed up."

"Wait! What?"

Nodding with her eyes wide, Penny explained, "Yeah, she busted right in my bedroom door just as we were about..."

Quickly cutting her off Charlotte, questioned, "Your mom came to our apartment?"
Hesitant, Penny nodded.

"Did she say anything about the wedding? Is she coming?"

There was a long pause before Penny answered, "She mostly just fussed at me and Braden."

"Oh, Okay..."

"Sorry." Penny genuinely assured, walking to turn off the lights.
Following her, Charlotte wondered if Auggie knew his mom had come by and if he did, why wouldn't he tell her?

Chapter 13

Braden was sitting in the manager's office of The Dog House when Charlotte walked in to get her night started. Instead of being seated in the chair facing the desk, he sat on the one right inside the door.

After giving him a quick once over, Charlotte shook her head at him as she walked to her desk.

"What's up?"

Shrugging, he replied, "Auggie sent me in here."

Trying her best not to laugh, Charlotte asked, "He put you in a time out?"

"Can't you lift the sex ban before he actually bites someone's head clean off?" He replied with a smirk.

"Did he seriously send you back here to talk me into having sex with him?" She snapped.

With a wide smile and a laugh, Braden swore, "Hey, I'm just tryin' to keep all us innocent bystanders safe."

"Champion of the people sorta thing?" Charlotte laughed.

"Somethin' like that."

Rolling her eyes, she sat down behind her desk and flipped her computer on.

When an hour went by and he was still sitting by the door in her office, Charlotte thought it might be nice to talk to him. Although she had known him for a while now and he was basically living on her couch, not once had there been a real conversation between the two of them.

Standing up behind her desk, she walked to the chair that sat in front of it and took a seat.

"So, how's it going?"

"How's what going?" He question, appearing confused.

"Life, I guess."

Braden's usual careless demeanor was replaced by a somber one as he shrugged and stared at the floor.

"Do you need someone to talk to?"

With an appreciative yet dismissive glance, he shook his head answering, "I can't talk to you."

"Not me." Charlotte agreed, almost laughing before suggesting, "You should talk to your brother."

"Yea, sure." He sarcastically replied.

"He's worried about you."

Standing up out of his chair, he took a step towards her as if he was about to argue then took a deep breath and stepped back.

Leaning his back against the door, he folded his arms in front of his chest and admitted, "I know he is."

"So talk to him." She urged.

Shaking his head, he relaxed his arms, dropped them at his sides and shared, "He doesn't understand."

"Isn't that the point of talking about something?"

Serious in expression, he replied, "It's not in him to understand."

Charlotte knew Auggie wasn't the most understanding person. Regardless of how he would approach whatever Braden's problem was, she knew he loved his brother.

As she started to press the issue of them talking, Braden informed, "Everyone in this family is doing exactly what they were always meant to do. Except me."

Feeling as though he was just having a pity party for himself, Charlotte stood up and advised, "Stop letting people take who you are away from you then."

Glancing up at the ceiling, Braden nodded before explaining, "That's the part that no one understands. Every cord I ever played is a moment and all the memories I have from it I don't want."

"So, go make new memories instead of punishing yourself?"

"With who?" Braden asked in a strained voice before saying, "Maybe not everyone has a purpose," as he reached for the door knob.

Charlotte's heart started to ache for him as she offered, "Maybe you just haven't found it yet."

A humorless smile spread across his face as he replied, "Or maybe I have and it belongs to someone else."

Caught off guard by his statement, Charlotte was just about to ask what he meant by that when Auggie opened the door and walked in.

Pausing for a moment, Auggie scowled between the two of them before stepping all the way into the room.

Turning to Braden, he informed, "Pat's out there."

"What's he doing here?" Braden asked, appearing surprised.

With a shrug of his shoulders, Auggie replied, "Said he's lookin' for you."

Braden nodded as he turned and walked out.

"Who's Pat?"

"Ol' friend of Braden's." Auggie replied before asking, "Was I interrupting?"

Rolling her eyes, Charlotte laughed.

He smiled at her, taking a step closer before reaching out to take her hand.

"Ten days."

Squeezing his hand, Charlotte smiled back and wrapped an arm around his waist.

The position they were now in, reminded her of the last two items on her checklist, prompting her to say, "The dance."

"You wanna dance?"

Shaking her head at him, she corrected, "I just remembered, I haven't picked a song for our first dance or the ceremony."

Letting go of her hand, he slid his arms around her.

Leaning his forehead to hers, he offered, "I already picked them."

In disbelief, she blurted, "Really? When?"

"Last month." He replied in a low tone while brushing his lips against hers.

The corner of her mouth curled into a smile as she said, "Why didn't you tell me?"

"I didn't want you to know." He answered kissing across her jaw.

Charlotte let out a soft sigh as she whispered, "Ten days."

Auggie nodded into her cheek before kissing down the side of her neck, then back up to her lips.

Chapter 14

Waking up to a text message from Charlotte that let him know she would be shopping with Liv and Penny all day before meeting him out at Kieran's, freed up a good bit of the day for Auggie to tend to a few post wedding related things before his bachelor party.

Without a whole lot of guidance, growing up in the romance department, Auggie spent most of the day wandering around The Store trying to pick out things he thought Charlotte might like. The idea he had come up with to make their first time as a married couple special, he knew was a good one, but he wasn't exactly sure how to pull it off. Just as he started to get frustrated with himself for not being able to figure it out, he turned a corner into home decor and was inspired.

Auggie pulled up to Kieran's feeling proud of himself. In one week from tomorrow, he was going to marry a woman he knew was going to be just as impossible to live with as she was to live without, then he was going to show her the definition of special with a hell yeah, damn straight Auggie's the mother effin' man.

As soon as he got out of his truck and reached the porch, Kieran stepped outside.

"Awfully chipper for a man about to meet his demise, aren't ya?" He laughed.

"Hell yeah, I'm goin' down a happy man."

Kieran smiled as if he were still joking but Auggie caught the seriousness of his tone as he replied, "Damn shame, I always thought you knew better than the rest of us."

There was no more humor in him as he asked, "You gotta problem?"

Tilting his head to the side, Kieran questioned, "Do you?"

With a hard scowl, Auggie replied, "If you got somethin' to say, say it."

Holding his hands out to his sides, he shook his head saying, "No problems here."

"You sure?"

Kieran stared at him for a minute before walking to the porch swing and sitting down.

Following him, Auggie took the chair next to the swing and waited for Kieran to answer.

"You ever have a thought that gets in your head and you can't get it out? It just digs itself deeper, gnawing at you as it grows?"

Instantly, the thought of Charlotte with his brother Will entered his mind.

"Yea, I do."

Nodding, Kieran shared, "I can't sleep next to her. Every night I wait for her to fall asleep.

Then, I stare at her, wondering why the hell I married her."

Auggie was so startled by what his cousin said, he felt like he'd been slapped.

"And I ask myself, if I believe in the legacy, my legacy, then why did I do it. I love her, I know I do. But I can't help thinking if she's the one, I would have taken her mark instead of doing what I did."

"You messin' around on Liv?" Auggie questioned, ready to take a swing the second he said 'yes'.

"Nah, but that's another thing. I think it's more 'cause I'm faithful then I don't want anyone else."

"What the hell is wrong with you?" Auggie growled, finding himself well past irritated with Kieran.

"I've come too far to go back and it's suffocating me."

Standing up, Auggie barked, "No, you're a self-absorbed dick who needs his ass kicked for not appreciating having the woman you do."

On his feet too, Kieran griped, "Sell that self-righteousness to someone who doesn't know you lied about who drew out your mark."

"I lied to spare Charlotte's feelings not because I needed a plan b in case things don't work out."

An unexpected smile formed on Kieran's face as he patted Auggie on the back saying, "Don't get all pissy. You know me."

Glaring at his cousin, Auggie wondered if he really did, because nothing he had just said sounded like it came from his family.

"Let's get about celebrating one of your last nights as a free man."

Just so there were no misunderstandings between them, Auggie replied, "My last night as a free man was the one before I met her."

Chapter 15

For the first time in Auggie's life, he didn't want to be at his cousin's house. He didn't care about freedom or being a bachelor. If he did, he sure as hell wouldn't have proposed to Charlotte. As he glanced around the porch at the company he was keeping, Kieran, his dumbass brother Braden, and Penny's boyfriend Seth, he started to wonder why he was there in the first place.

He was six beers into the evening when he decided as soon as Charlotte got there, they would leave.

Pulling his cell phone out of his pocket, he started to text her when he heard Braden gripe, "This is the lamest bachelor party in the history of bachelor parties."

"Take off then." Auggie suggested without looking in his direction.

For whatever reason, Seth felt the need to speak up on Auggie's behalf.

"Probably because this isn't a real bachelor party, it's celebrating him about to get married."

Glaring at Seth, Auggie knew he was right but still, he didn't need some guy that was trying to get down with his little sister, defending the lameness of the evening.

"What the hell do we do for that then?" Braden questioned before Kieran suggested, "Get drunk and shoot each other?"

Braden's face lit up while Seth's fell into a fearful expression as he blurted, "What?"

Glancing at the three of them as Kieran pressed, "What do ya say Auggs?" He nodded.

"Hell yeah!" Auggie agreed, thinking I'd like to shoot every damn one of you.

Dusting off a large box in the shed behind the house before opening it, Kieran looked around before stopping and turning to Auggie.

"You know what I was sayin' before, I was just talkin' outta my ass."

Crossing his arms across his chest, Auggie agreed, "Damn right, you were."

"I have regrets. And your brother showing up with the damn tattoo...it's screwin' with me. Knowing I marked him." Stopping to shake his head at himself, Kieran continued, "I shoulda told him no."

With a heavy sigh, Auggie shared, "Should have, but you didn't. Everything else that's going on in your head though, that's on you."

"I wanna believe that Auggs, but..."

Braden's voice interrupted Kieran and startled them both as he shouted, "You sure Liv's not gonna get pissed we brought her furniture out here?"

Glancing at Auggie, Kieran hollered back, "Nope, why do you think I had you do it."

Hearing Braden curse Kieran as he walked off, Auggie started to laugh.

"We good?" Kieran questioned holding his hand out.

Nodding, Auggie shook his hand before helping him with the box of paintball guns.

Lying on his stomach behind a mattress, propped against a large tree, Auggie waited for his brother to peek out from behind the couch far enough for him to catch him in the shoulder. Just as he was aimed and ready, a pair of headlights shown bright coming up the gravel driveway causing Braden to pull back out of sight.

The second Charlotte's car stopped, Liv jumped out hollering. While Kieran promised to buy her a new couch, Seth ran across from out of nowhere announcing that Penny was his hostage.

Laughing when Braden shouted, "She's not a hostage if you're the only one that wants her." Auggie caught sight of Charlotte.

Standing there with her back to him, in navy blue heals and a tan skirt that showed more of her legs than he felt anyone other than him should see, he couldn't resist the moment. Drawing in a deep breath, he slowly blew it out and pulled the trigger.

The blue paintball splatter on the back of her skirt was immediately followed by a yelp.

"Augustus Caffrey!" She shouted, swinging around and glaring right at him.

He wanted to laugh, but the look on her face warned him, he'd better run instead. Dropping his gun, he hopped up and took off around the side of the house, hearing her not far behind him.

Years of hide and seek back when they were kids and when Kieran's parent's owned the farmhouse, gave Auggie the advantage over Charlotte in the dark. He watched her slowly glance around searching for him. As soon as she was close enough, he reached out and grabbed her, pulling her behind pallets of bricks stacked almost as high as the roof.

"You shot me in the ass!" Charlotte growled at him as she tried to elbow her way out of his arms.

Laughing, he held her tighter offering, "Want me to kiss it and make it better?"

Clearly not amused, she fussed, "That hurt, you jackass."

Trying to keep his laughter at bay now, Auggie assured, "I'm sorry, I figured I was far enough away, that it would just sting a little."

"Well, it stings a whole hell of a lot more than a little." She insisted as she smacked him in the back of his head.

Unable to keep from smiling, Auggie reached down and slid his hand up the back of her thigh and under her skirt.

"Better?" he asked gently rubbing her wounded behind.

Relaxing in his arms, Charlotte closed her eyes.

Pushing her back against the pallet of bricks, Auggie heard her sigh as she leaned her forehead onto his chest. It was dark and the thought that no one would see or hear them provoked him to move his other hand up the back of her skirt.

"Seven days." She whimpered, reminding him, he was about to take things too far.

Letting go of her, Auggie remained close, swearing, "It's a date."

Chapter 16

Five days before the wedding, things slowly started to go wrong. Penny and Seth broke up and although Charlotte took Penny's side, because that's what best friends do, she realized Penny could be just as stubborn as her big brother. When convincing her to hear Seth out didn't work, Charlotte tried to talk Auggie into stepping in, but all that was accomplished was that there was a pretty lengthy argument between Charlotte and her ass of a soon to be husband.

Her only hope was talking Braden into getting Seth to go talk to Auggie, which to no surprise he agreed to, but at the same time she could tell he was still struggling with his own problems.

Now with just two days until the I do's and Auggie's youngest brother Ailin and his wife Sophia down for the wedding, Charlotte could feel herself cracking under the pressure of the upcoming event and the stress of everything that was going on around her as she stood in the kitchen at Ren's house.

Charlotte made sure there was as much distance between her and Sophia as possible. She still couldn't stand her, so while Sophia sat on the couch in the living room with Penny, no doubt making her feel worse than she already was, Charlotte stayed in the kitchen watching the clock until it was time to go.

She only had thirty minutes left to endure when she turned and saw Auggie walking into the kitchen, carrying his niece Keylee.

It occurred to her she was fixing to be her niece too as Auggie said, "There's Aunt Charlotte," with a smile.

Forcing a smile, Charlotte replied, "She really seems to like you."

Happily nodding, he coaxed, "Say 'hi' to Aunt Charlotte."

Giving her a little wave, Charlotte started to smile when Jackson stepped in the room.

"Hey, can you give me a hand?"

Auggie answered, "Sure," before handing Keylee over to Charlotte.

It happened so fast, she didn't even have a chance to protest.

Bracing herself against the counter, Keylee was a little heavier than she appeared and the way she was squirming made Charlotte afraid that she would drop her.

"No, no, he'll be right back. Okay?" She tried reasoning with the almost one year old who seemed insistent on flailing her arms and legs around.

Looking around for assistance, no one was even paying attention.

"Keylee, please." She begged trying to get her under control.

At that moment, Keylee must have realized Auggie was nowhere to be found and she was stuck with Charlotte.

Scrunching her entire face up as if she was going to cry, Charlotte couldn't help laughing as she shared, "Well that's an ugly little expression." Keylee's expression instantly went blank and then a little baby scowl formed between her light brown eyebrows.

"Oh, no. You are going to be all kinds of trouble aren't you." She laughed, curling the side of her mouth into a smile.

Charlotte's smile earned her a wide giggly one from Keylee.

"I bet you're going to be somethin' else when you grow up." She continued, smiling wider at her.

Another giggle from Keylee and Charlotte couldn't help giving her a little squeeze.

As she reached out, grabbing strands of Charlotte's hair off of her shoulder, Charlotte thought she inherited the best Caffrey traits. She looked just like Ailin, scowled like Auggie, smiled just like Braden and there was no doubt she would be beautiful just like Penny. Then laughing to herself, she mentally cautioned, 'I hope you don't act like your mother.'

Keylee started to squirm again, causing Charlotte to turn around. An unusual feeling settled in the pit of her stomach when she realized Auggie had been standing there watching them with a smile on his face. When she saw the look in his eyes, whatever the feeling had been, changed. She was certain he wanted something that she couldn't give him.

Auggie was in such a good mood, it was actually starting to make Charlotte sick. It wasn't as if she wanted him to be in a bad mood, but his happiness was making her feel bad.

As soon as they walked in the back door of The Dog House, he pulled her to him, saying, "Two days."

All of the sudden Charlotte felt like she was about to cry. Holding onto him tight, she nodded against his shoulder.

His hold tightened also as he asked, "What's wrong?"

Taking a deep breath, Charlotte pulled away, stating, "I have been up front with you from the beginning."

Concern immediately spread across Auggie's face as he replied, "Okay?"

"So I would appreciate it if you would be upfront with me."

"Okay?" He repeated a bit slower as confusion took over his concern.

He always had to be so damn frustrating.

"Okay? That's all you have to say?"

"Was there a question somewhere in there I missed or are you just want me to start confessin' stuff?"

With a loud huff, Charlotte tugged the bottom of her shirt and swiftly walked to her office, slamming the door behind her.

She didn't have time to make it behind her desk, when the door flew open.

Storming into the room, Auggie growled, "You listen hear woman, we are getting married day after tomorrow so either you tell me what you think I've done or save your imaginary reason's to argue 'til after the wedding 'cause I haven't made it this far for you to start givin' me hell now."

Furious with him, she fussed, "Admit it, you want kids."

"What in the hell? Where did you get that from?"

Narrowing her eyes at him, she replied, "I saw the way you were smiling at me and Keylee."

"You have got to be the craziest, crazy ass woman on earth!"

"Is that right?"

"Ya damn right, that's right. It couldn't of been because you were holding my niece and it was cute seeing y'all together. But I'll sure as hell keep a straight face from now until the wedding so I can wait out the last two days in peace."

Seeing reason, but unwilling to give up the fight quite yet, she snapped, "Oh, please tell me how hard it's been to make it this far."

Taking a step closer to her, Auggie griped, "I've been walkin' around for the last month with it so hard, I can touch you with it from two feet away."

"Really? Two feet?" Charlotte questioned with a slight smirk.

A hint of a smile threatened to break through as he added, "And a quarter."

Glancing down, she curled the corner of her mouth into a smile before looking back up at him as he smiled back giving her a nod of assurance.

Chapter 17

A steady stream of customers and congratulations kept Auggie busy behind the bar for most of the night. It was good having Kieran and Liv at the bar together. When Penny showed up with Braden, they squeezed in next to Liv and nothing but laugher came from that end of the bar even after the doors were locked.

Closing up the bar Auggie smiled to himself, knowing the next time he opened it, he would be a married man. One more day. Never in his life, before Charlotte, would he have believed how happy something like that would make him.

Stepping into the kitchen, he thought about how seeing Charlotte with Keylee made him feel. It was hard to explain, especially to himself, since he never thought about having kids of his own. Something about the way she was holding her and the look on her face as she smiled at his niece that caused his mind to wonder. Taking a moment before walking back into the main area of the bar, he let his thoughts drift to the impossible.

It wasn't a kid thing, especially when Caffrey family babies were plentiful and there was always a new one popping out. It was a Charlotte thing. Making babies with someone wasn't something he would have considered particularly thrilling, but when he imagined Charlotte holding one with fiery red hair and her blue eyes, his chest involuntarily started to swell.

Shaking off a smile as he walked back into the main area of the bar, Auggie stopped and stared at his brother. Trying to figure out what had happened in the minute he stepped away, He watched Braden moving towards Kieran with Liv in between them.

"What's your drunk ass gonna do?" Kieran mocked as he stood up tall in front of Braden.

"Little help here, Auggs?" Liv snapped, noticing he had walked back in.

"Nah, let's see what he's got." Kieran taunted, provoking Braden to lunge at him.

Quickly grabbing Braden from behind, Auggie held him back, warning, "Knock it off."

With heavy breath, Braden shared, "He's been lying to Penny this whole time."

Auggie immediately glared at Kieran as he said, "It's my shop."

Right then and there Auggie knew Penny's apprenticeship was pointless.

He was just as angry with Kieran as Braden seemed to be, but at the same time, Penny was in the back and she already had a broken heart, she didn't need to find out about this too.

"Let it go." Auggie advised Branden before Kieran took a step closer saying, "Come on, little boy."

"I said, knock it off." Auggie growled directly at Kieran at the same time Liv planted her hands against his chest shouting, "Stop it!"

Braden started to shout, "You're a sorry ass mother f..." When Liv cut him off, agreeing, "Yeah, that's a dirty thing to do."

Looking down at his wife, Kieran barked, "Why ya takin' his side?"

"You're wrong for making her think..."

"Liv!" Auggie snapped, seeing Penny walk up.

Stepping closer to them, Penny hesitantly asked, "What am I missing?"
All Auggie could do was stare at the confused expression on his sisters face.

Allowing Braden to jerk away, Auggie couldn't say a word. There was no way he was going to be the one to hurt her.

Much to his relief, Braden griped, "Nothin' Pen, let's go," as he stepped toward her.

Shaking her head at him, she looked at all of them asking, "This is about me?"

Braden nodded, saying, "Guess no one else is man enough, I'll tell you."

"Braden!" Auggie snapped before Braden turned to him hollering, "You should be just as mad as I am."

Auggie instantly yelled back, "I'm not gonna tell the man what he can and can't do in his shop."

"Did Penny say that to you when mom refused to draw out your tattoo or did..." Braden started to shout but was cut off when Auggie heard Charlotte question, "What?"
Panic and anger instantly filled him.

Grabbing the front of his brother's shirt, Auggie was seconds away from knocking Braden out when Charlotte shoved Braden away and stood in front of him.

"She refused?" She questioned with an angry glare.

"Lotte..."Auggie started before Charlotte narrowed her eye at him, fussing, "I cannot believe you."
Furious with Braden, he pointed directly at him and swore, "Your dumbass is out of the wedding."

Charlotte quickly assured, "No, you're not." Then went on to snap at Auggie, "No, he's not."

"The hell he's not." Auggie growled in frustration.

"Do you wanna marry me?"
Wondering what the hell kind of a question was that, Auggie nodded.

"Then he's in the wedding." Charlotte informed before turning and heading out of the room.

"Where are you going?"

"To see your mother!" Charlotte snapped, causing Auggie to stop dead in his tracks.

One damn day was all he had left and dumbass Braden couldn't keep his mouth shut.

"I better not see your ass before three on Saturday." Auggie warned his brother.

Pushing through the swinging doors, he took off after Charlotte.

Chapter 18

Charlotte counted back from ten after each loud knock on Sarah Caffrey's door. She knew Auggie wouldn't be right behind her. She took care of that by throwing his keys down the alley behind the bar when he tried to stop her. But, he would eventually find them and if this woman didn't hurry up and open the door, she would never get the answer she came for.

After ten minutes of banging on the door, Charlotte noticed the curtain on the front window move.

"Mrs. Caffrey, it's Charlotte!" She started before asking, "Can I speak with you?"

The door barely cracked open as she heard Auggie's mother question, "Charlotte who?"
Taking a slow deep breath, Charlotte mentally questioned, 'How many Charlotte's knock on her door in the middle of the night?'.

"Your son's fiancée."

Pulling the door open a little farther, Sarah stated, "You're not welcome in my house."

Nodding, Charlotte took a step back and glanced around assuring, "I can say what I need to say on the porch."
Sarah quickly swung the front door open and stepped out.

It was hard for Charlotte to stay angry when Auggie's mom looked so much like Penny. Sarah had quite a few more years on her than her daughter but every bit of her was simply an older version, right down to her auburn hair that was held in a long braid, hanging over her shoulder.

Placing her hand on her hip, Sarah shot Charlotte a hard glare.

"I feel sorry for the Roberts'."

"Excuse me?" Charlotte snapped, before reminding herself she needed to at least try to be respectful towards Auggie's mother.

"I'm sure they raised you better."

Mentally counting back from ten in her head, Charlotte replied, "Well, I'm sure they appreciate that."

"Doubtful." Sarah mumbled before griping, "Let's hear it."

Charlotte paused, realizing now that she was face to face with the woman she was sure hated her, this wasn't about Sarah.

Sarah had made her feelings about Charlotte known and clear from the beginning. Regardless of whether she was right or wrong in her assumptions about Charlotte, she was honest. Charlotte could respect that.

It wasn't Sarah she had an issue with at all, it was Auggie.

"I apologize for coming out here so late and waking you up."

Scowling at her, Sarah griped, "Seems a little strange to me that you would cause something to apologize for."

"I don't have a problem with you."

"And you assume I have a problem with you?"

"Don't you?"

Sarah's face held a stern expression as she replied, "The problem I have is that one day the novelty of my son will wear off for you."

Shaking her head, Charlotte swore, "I'm in love with him."

"At the moment you are, but as soon as you're stuck home with kids and responsibility while he spends every night at the bar..."

As Auggie's truck pulled onto the gravel driveway interrupting her, Charlotte let out a frustrated groan.

Charlotte noticed Sarah shake her head as Auggie swiftly making his way to the porch.

"Ma, I need to talk to Charlotte." He insisted.

"Son, I don't think she came here to talk to you."

"I didn't." Charlotte confirmed with a harsh glare.

Stepping closer to her, Charlotte could tell Auggie was remorseful as he apologized, "Lotte, I'm sorry."

Before Charlotte could respond, Sarah snapped, "Are the two of you still getting married?"

"Yes." They replied in unison.

Appearing put out, she fussed, "Then get off my porch, go home and I will see ya'll Saturday."

Surprised, not by being told to leave but that she was coming to the wedding, Charlotte blurted, "You will?"

Sarah turned and opened her front door before looking back at her.

"What kind of mother would I be, if I wasn't there to see my son get married?" Sarah scolded before stepping into the house and slamming the front door behind her.

As Charlotte stared at the door, even though their conversation was brief, she understood why Sarah disliked her.

It was fear. She didn't want her son to get hurt. Sarah was afraid for him. In a way, it made Charlotte feel good. It meant even his mom could see how much Auggie loved her. But on the other side of that, was a man, who in spite of all his love, lied to her.

Charlotte could feel Auggie staring at her as she stepped off the porch.

"You shouldn't have lied to me." She whispered, making her way out to her car.

Chapter 19

The wedding party was gathered outside at his Uncle Brennan's place for the wedding rehearsal and Charlotte seemed angrier with Auggie than she was the night before. Thanks to Braden not showing up for the rehearsal, she now had something new to be mad at him for.

Auggie followed Charlotte out to her car, she had walked off on him one too many times, and he was getting pretty aggravated himself.

"Would ya stop for a minute!" Auggie griped, trying to catch up with her.

Shaking her head, she continued to her car.

When Charlotte reached her car, Auggie stepped directly behind her, sliding his hands around hers.

She started to hold his hands then pulled away, asking, "How many times am I supposed to forgive you."

"As many as it takes to keep us together." Auggie replied, suddenly feeling panic rising in his chest.

Turning, Charlotte looked into his eyes and stated, "I don't know what's worse. That I'm not worth your honesty or that you'd rather lie then talk to me."

"Lotte..."

"You swore nothing would come between us and I believed you. I believed you when you told me there was no more you and me, only us."

With an anguished expression on his face, Auggie lifted his hands to the sides of her face asking, "And now you don't?"

"It's you that doesn't believe in us."

Shaking his head in confusion, Auggie replied, "I do."

"Then why lie to me?" Charlotte asked, her eyes searching his for the truth.

He looked into her eyes, at the time he had a reason, but at the moment it didn't make sense.

Sliding away from him, Charlotte nodded.

"I'm sure about us." She swore before her voice cracked as she suggested, "If you're not, don't even bother showing up tomorrow."

A sharp pain twisted in Auggie's chest before settling in his stomach causing him to take a step back.

"You don't want to get married?"

Opening her car door, he could see tears pool in her eyes as she replied, "I don't want to wake up one day and have to pretend to be someone I'm not because you suddenly don't want me anymore."

~

Auggie sat alone in The Dog House with a bottle of whiskey, keeping the bottom of his glass filled as he sipped it, thinking about what Charlotte said. He knew she was talking about Kieran and Liv. The more he drank, the more he compared himself to his cousin.

Refusing to believe there was a similarity there, Auggie recalled when Kieran chose his own mark over Liv's.

Wearing a proud expression, Kieran puffed his chest in Auggie's direction.

"What'd ya think?"

Eyeing the mark on the left side of his cousin's chest, Auggie laughed, "It might be time for your ol' man to retire."

"Why?" Kieran asked, looking down at his own chest.

"'Cause that doesn't look like a lily to me."

Breathing a sigh of relief, Kieran slapped Auggie's shoulder, informing, "I had Sarah change it."

"You serious?" Auggie questioned, finding it hard to believe, given how committed his cousin was to his legacy.

"I love Liv. Have since the first time I saw her. But, man, I was sittin' there at your mom's and all these 'what ifs' kept gettin' me."

"She's gonna be pissed. You know that right?"

With a quick nod, Kieran shared, "She was. Swore it's 'cause Sarah hates her."

Giving him a slight shove, Auggie griped, "What the hell?"

"What? Your mom does hate her and besides, this one's more my style."

Growing disappointed with him, Auggie asked, "And when she finds out?"

"How's she gonna know?"

Shaking his head, Auggie replied, "For what it's worth, you're wrong for doin' that. Liv's cool as hell."

"She is, isn't she." Kieran agreed with a wide smile before saying, "We'll see how you handle the nail in your coffin, when your day comes."

"Ain't happenin.'"

Kieran rolled his eyes and laughed, "Admit it, you'd do the same."

"You're messin' with tradition. It's gonna bite you in the ass one day."

"What can I say, cousin, Liv's badass but it never hurts to have a plan b."

"If you say so. Won't matter for me. There's not a woman on earth bad enough to own me."

Scowling into his glass of whiskey, Auggie shook his head at himself. Why couldn't he have inherited some wisdom from his dad? If he were here, they could share the bottle while Gus imparted one of his sayings that would make everything alright.

As Auggie sat there thinking about his dad, his family and the woman he loved, he heard the doors open.

"Bar's closed." He informed, not caring who it was as long as they left.

"I want to be with Penny." Seth announced, sounding like his life depended on it.

"Good for you." He replied, taking a sip of his whiskey.

"What do I do?"

Surprised at how quickly the answer came to him, Auggie knew exactly what Seth should do.

Chapter 20

Staring at her cell phone, Charlotte thought about calling Auggie before she fell asleep and again when she woke up. She expected at least a text message from him assuring her he would show up for the wedding. With a loud huff, she slid out of bed, hoping the day would go as planned. After all, Auggie didn't have the best track record when it came to important events.

Before Charlotte made it to the bathroom, her bedroom door flew open.

By the time the door slammed shut Silvia was in her face, questioning, "Have you heard from Braden? He's still coming, right?"

Taking a step back, Charlotte fussed, "Seriously! Stop!"

Silvia frowned, instantly pouting as she griped, "You're in a mood."

"Could it be because my sister has no manners?"

Still pouting with persistence, Silvia replied, "Please? Tell me he's coming."

Narrowing her eyes at her sister, Charlotte stated, "Just get out."

"Uhh... Fine! You're so selfish." Silvia complained as she left the room.

'Unbelievable.' Charlotte thought as she finally made it to her bathroom.

Checking her cell phone again, now that she was dressed, the fact that Auggie still had not called or sent her a text message was starting to bother her. What if he didn't show up? The thought made her uneasy, until irritation set in. It was a much more manageable emotion than fear. Choosing to focus on what a jackass her soon to be husband was, helped alleviate the uncertainty of how the day would turn out.

She stopped to look at herself in the mirror and read the words off of the shirt that she was wearing, 'I CAN'T KEEP CALM, I'M GETTING MARRIED.' After counting back from ten in her head, Charlotte thought; 'You better have picked one hell of a wedding song, Augustus,' and walked out of her room.

~

Charlotte sat on a stool inside her wedding preparation tent, listening to the voices and various sounds of everyone outside the tent setting up. Taking slow deep breaths, she tried not to panic. No one had seen or heard from Auggie since the night before.

Chapter 21

Bumping the side of his fist against the top of the table Seth was passed out under, Auggie heard him quickly sit up and bang his head underneath it.

"You alright?"
Groaning his reply, Seth dragged himself out from under the table.
In all the nights Auggie spent drinking, he had never seen anyone actually drink themselves under a table.

Climbing into a chair, Seth laid his head down on the table, saying, "I feel like death."

"Ya look like it too." He teased before advising, "Go home and shower. Tea, not coffee, take aspirin, a nap and then another shower and you should be good."

Seth cringed as he looked up at Auggie saying, "That was...specific."

"Best of luck to ya." He added, grabbing a bottle of Guinness off of the bar.

~

Auggie glanced into the rearview mirror at his suit jacket and tie hanging in the back seat of his truck. Why he'd waited so long to do this he wasn't sure, but timing is everything and today felt right. Grabbing the beer out of his console, he opened the door and got out.

Walking across the grass, Auggie stopped next to a marble marker. He leaned down and placed the Guinness next to his brother's headstone and smiled.

"I won't keep ya, Will. I got somewhere to be." He shared before informing, "Gettin' married today."

Running his hand down the front of his beard, he took a moment to laugh at himself.

"You probably already knew that, I'm not sure how all this works. Point is, there's somethin' I have to say to you."

Nodding at the silence of the cemetery, Auggie continued.

"Guess you were wondering when I'd figure out that you set us up. I hope you know she's gonna give me hell for the rest of my life." Stopping to smile he acknowledged, "But I'm a better man for it."

Pausing, he took a deep breath.

"Anyway, what I came out here to say was... Thank you. Thank you for bringing Charlotte into my life. I love ya, brother."

Auggie took a step back and nodded again before turning and walking to his truck.

Back in his truck, Auggie headed out to his uncle Brennen's. With his heart thundering in his chest, he was about to be married and no one, not even he, was going to ruin the day.

Chapter 22

Stepping out of the barn, on the far end of Brennen's property, Auggie stopped and looked around. He recalled the day he took Charlotte out to tend to the peacocks. Half teasing in intent, he remembered her long sexy legs awkwardly maneuvering the rubber boots she had on, the way she gazed at the pretty birds that didn't come close to how beautiful she was, and how stunning her blue eyes were the first time he really looked into them. No way in hell was he going to tell her she needed to keep her hands to herself this time.

As Auggie's cell phone vibrated in his slacks, he figured it was time to make his way to his tent and get ready. Pulling his phone out, he saw a text from Penny.

P: What is the matter with you?

Confused, he texted her back.

A: What?

P: Where are you?

A: At the barn. Why?

Hopping in his truck, Auggie waited for her to text back.

P: Charlotte is freaking out! She thinks you're not going to show up.

Firing up his engine, he couldn't stop himself from smiling.

A: On my way.

~

With the assurance that Auggie had arrived, Charlotte felt confident enough to slip her shoes on. She had waited until she was sure he was there before committing to her Marc Defang, open toe peacock blue diamond frost heels.

Glancing over at Amila and Penny, she smiled, lifting the hem of her wedding gown. Charlotte started to show off her stunning heels, when she noticed something sparkle by her foot. Reaching down, she picked up a bobby pin that had obviously fallen out of her hair. As she stood upright, a long piece of gathered hair, that it had been holding, fell across her face.

Panic instantly set in.

"What if he showed up to tell everyone the wedding's off?"

Charlotte watched as Penny frowned at her phone and whispered something to Amila before leaving the tent.

"He changed his mind didn't he?"

A soft smile formed on Amila's face as she stepped to Charlotte assuring, "Honey, you need to calm down."

Shaking her head, she swore, "I can't."

Amila continued to smile as she lifted the hair out of Charlotte's face and replaced the bobby pin asking, "If you're having second thoughts or you're not sure..."

On the verge of tears, Charlotte confessed, "I'm afraid. I love him. If it ever ends... I..."

Nodding, Amila placed her hand on Charlotte's shoulder imparting, "I don't think Auggie's the type of man that would be here if he didn't feel exactly the same way."

Charlotte smiled, starting to feel better.

Giving her a light squeeze, Amila shared, "Now, I have to go see if we left your garter in the car. You can't get married without that. Talk about bad luck."

"What?" Charlotte blurted, as Amila left the tent.

~

Penny stood in front of Auggie with her hand on her hip and a 'what do you want me to do' expression on her face.

"I want him in here." He assured, thinking maybe she hadn't made that part clear.

"I told him that."

"Is he gonna stand up there with me?" Auggie questioned, aggravated at the way his brother was behaving.

Shrugging, Penny replied, "He's wearing his tux so I imagine, but if you wanna know, you go talk to Braden. I've got to get back to Charlotte."

"Thanks, Pen." He said as she waved her hand behind her head and walked out.

Shaking his head with a deep scowl, he started to head out and look for Braden, when his mom walked in.

"Sit down and give me your shoes." She ordered without so much as a smile.

"I'm still gonna marry her, whether you take my shoes or not, Ma." He replied with a slight smile.

Pursing her lips at him, Sarah swatted Auggie on the arm saying, "I realize that, son."
Doing as he was told, he watched Sarah dust the bottom of his shoes off as he handed them to her.

Handing his dress shoes over to Ailin, Auggie's mom gave Kieran two small stickers. Kieran gave Sarah a strange look as Ailin shook his head and started to laugh.

"Go on, help him." Sarah told Kieran before looking at Auggie saying, "You've never half-assed anything in your entire life. Don't start now."
Nodding, Auggie smiled at his mom as she kissed the side of his head before exiting just as abruptly as she entered.

Forgetting about Braden for the moment, Auggie looked over to his brother and cousin to see what they were doing to his shoes. Both wore wide smiles as they showed him the soles. *'She's'* was on one and *'Mine'* was on the other. Shaking his head, he couldn't help laughing.

Chapter 23

Charlotte stood with her arm hooked around Emerson's, waiting to make her way down the aisle.

Looking down at her with a compassionate smile, Emerson asked, "Are you alright?"
Charlotte nodded, realizing her feather bouquet was shaking in her hands.

Emerson cleared his throat as he shared, "I'm proud to have had some small part in the woman that you have become. I consider it an honor to give you away today."
Feeling tears well in her eyes at his words, Charlotte opened her mouth to reply but couldn't when she heard the music start to play.

Her heart swelled in her chest as a warm sensation travelled throughout her entire body.
'I can hear her heart beat from a thousand miles.'
Crazy Love by Brian McKnight was the song Auggie chose to be their wedding song.
'Hear the heavens open every time she smiles.'
Unable to stop herself she lunged forward.

"Whoa, there," Emerson laughed, pulling her back before informing, "Not yet."

All of Charlotte's anxiety was gone and replaced by an almost unbearable anticipation to be by Auggie's side. Every part of her being needed to be with him.

~

Standing up tall as he waited for Charlotte to make her way down the aisle and stand at his side, Auggie gave a quick nod at Kieran as he stood next to him. As Braden took his place next to his cousin, he noticed an unpleasant expression on his brother's face.

Wondering what the hell his problem was, Auggie stared at Braden. Barely noticing Ailin make his way over, he tapped Kieran on the arm and motioned for him to get Braden's attention.

"Hey." Auggie quietly snapped as Kieran nudged Braden.

Braden glared as Kieran took a step back and Auggie gave him a questioning look.

"Braden." Auggie bit out in a hushed tone.

Taking a step towards his brother, Braden whispered, "Like you give a damn."

"What the f..." Auggie started before he caught himself remembering where he was at, he swore, "You're my brother."

With a slight shove, Braden griped, "Not your best man though."

Auggie couldn't help shoving him back.

Instantly in his face, Braden gritted out, "Brother? If Will was here you'd of picked him." Before Auggie had a chance to say anything, Braden swung at him.

Tackling his brother to the ground, Auggie tried his best to not to fight Braden, but he wasn't about to get his ass kicked at his own wedding either. Barely avoiding getting punched in the eye, Auggie caught Braden's wrists pinning them to the ground and sat on him.

While Braden struggled to break free, the music stopped causing Auggie to look up. He swore his heart stopped beating for a full minute, the moment he saw Charlotte standing in front of him.

"Just another Caffrey family gathering." She declared, looking down at him.
Smiling wide, at the only woman on earth that could own him, Auggie let go of his brother and stood up.

~

Once everyone was back in their positions, Emerson continued to escort Charlotte down the aisle.

Charlotte found it hard to keep a straight face after Emerson laughed, 'This is the best wedding I've ever been to,' right before he gave her away. It also didn't help that it took him longer than necessary to compose himself enough to say; 'Her mother and I do.'

She could tell that Reverend Gary was a bit irritated by the way he was glaring at them.

He stated, "Dearly beloved we are..." Then stopped and stared directly at Penny.

Charlotte threw her hand over her mouth when she turned and saw Seth kissing Penny right there in front of everyone. Stunned by what was happening, Charlotte watched as Seth professed his love for Penny then took a knee and proposed to her.

In awe of their moment, Charlotte was thrilled for them.

Just as Seth stood, waiting for her answer, Auggie cleared his throat and said, "You know, when I said you had my blessing, this isn't what I meant."

Turning her focus to Auggie, Charlotte took his hand and kissed him on the cheek. Silently thanking him for this moment.

As Auggie smiled at her, Reverend Gary finally lost it.

Slamming his hand down on the altar, he shouted, "This is supposed to be a solemn occasion!"

Charlotte instantly burst into laughter, causing the Reverend's face to turn bright red.

"That's it! This is the last family wedding I'm doing!" He swore before snapping, "Auggie, you gonna marry her?"

Glaring at him, he replied, "Yes."

"Charlotte, you really want to marry into this?"

Smiling wider than she had thought possible, she answered, "Yes."

"Then kiss her, your married." He griped before stomping off saying, "I need a damn drink."

"I think we broke Reverend Gary." Braden blurted, causing everyone to start laughing.

Auggie wrapped his arms around her waist pulling her close as their laughter faded. Sliding her hands to the sides of his face, Charlotte brushed her thumbs against his beard.

"Kiss me."

She could feel Auggie's jaw tighten and his body tense as he held himself in reserve, placing one small soft kiss against her lips.

"Mrs. Caffrey." He stated, letting go of her and taking a slight step back.

"Yes?"

Caught off guard, Charlotte yelped as he swiftly picked her up and tossed her over his shoulder, assuring, "You're comin' with me."

Everyone stood and cheered their congratulations to them as he carried her. Doing her best to smile and wave as they made their way down the aisle, when they passed Liv she reached her hand out. Charlotte high-fived her, thinking 'Hell yeah!'.

Auggie set her down when they reached his truck.

"Are we going somewhere?"

"About a mile that way." He replied, pointing behind them before opening the passenger side door for her.

Surprised, Charlotte laughed, "You can't be serious."

"Oh, I'm serious." He stated before lifting her into the passenger seat of his truck.

"Augustus, we can't just leave." She shared, finding it difficult to be stern with him.

"This is our day. We can do whatever we want."

Chapter 24

Stopping his truck when they reached the old barn, Auggie could feel Charlotte staring at him. Without an explanation, he opened his door and got out. He tried his best to be serious and hold back a smile, finding it impossible as thoughts of her reaction to his surprise entered his mind.

After making his way around the front of his truck, Auggie opened the passenger door. He leaned in, sliding his hands around Charlotte hips as she turned to him.

"Are we going to see the peacocks?" She questioned as he lifted her out.

Shaking his head, he tugged her close, whispering, "Close your eyes."
A soft smile formed as she obeyed.

Auggie scooped Charlotte up off of her feet and carried her to the doors. Shifting her in his arms to open the door, he held her tight as he dragged it open.

"Keep 'em closed." He encouraged, kissing her on the cheek while stepping in and setting her back on her feet.

With eyes closed Charlotte asked, "What are you doing?"

Stepping back to look at her, he replied, "Making up for every time I let my pride get in the way."

Tilting her head down, Charlotte shared, "I have a surprise for you too."

"Mine first." He said, stepping up to the work bench.

Auggie struck a match and lit a lantern before carrying it with him as he closed the barn door.

Taking her hand in his, he carried the lantern, leading her to the back left corner of the old barn.

"Don't open yet." He warned, letting go of her hand and setting the lantern on a small table.

Proud of the way his surprise for her turned out, Auggie took a minute to make sure the queen size bed with a high square frame and sheer fabric netting draped over the top was perfect.

Back at Charlotte's side, he took her hand, saying, "Okay."

Watching her reaction carefully as she opened her eyes, he felt her smile in his heart as the glow from the lantern lit up her expression.

Appearing as though she had something to say but couldn't get the words out, she stood there staring at the bed.

"I'll take it down and bring it home tomorrow." He shared before suggesting, "I thought we could stay the night out here."

"This is ours?" She breathed with tears in her eyes.

Nodding at her, he took her face in his hands.

Auggie placed a long slow kiss against her lips before leaning his forehead to hers offering, "We can try it out right now."

"Help me with my dress." She urged as her face went flush.

Hating to pull away, even for a second, Auggie let go and stepped to the end of their bed.

All along he had planned on leaving it up to her, but at the same time, Auggie knew Charlotte wouldn't want to wait any longer than he did.

Picking up one of four hangers off of the chair he bought, that would also come home with them, he hung it from a partition he used to block the only window in the barn.

"I figured you would want us to look presentable for pictures at the reception," he informed, letting her know he had taken the time to think of everything.

There was a slight laugh to her tone as she replied, "You first."

Smiling at her he complied with her request.

Standing behind her in his boxers, Auggie ran his fingers across the white ink peacock feather tattooed across her shoulder blade. Slowly unzipping the back of her white satin wedding dress was torture as he forced himself to be thoughtful and take his time. When Charlotte held her arms high in the air, he gathered her dress in his hands and gently pulled it over her head.

Turning back to her once he had hung her dress next to his jacket, he wasn't sure if he was going to make it. Charlotte's skin, a pair of white satin panties and sparkly blue high heels almost pushed him right over the edge. Auggie gritted his teeth as his entire body flexed at the beautiful sight before him.

Charlotte slowly turned to face him. Placing her hands on his shoulders, she had a mischievous look in her eyes.

Glancing down between them, she uttered, "Two feet."

Moving his hands to her hips, he reminded, "And a quarter."

"That quarter's important." She laughed, as he nodded, saying, "Damn right."

Leaning in, he eagerly kissed her.

As Auggie held Charlotte against himself, the need to christen her under her new title provoked him to break their kiss.

Seeing her eyes flutter open as she sighed, he placed his hand against her cheek, vowing, "I, Augustus Carrick Caffrey, promise you, Charlotte Persephone Caffrey, the love I have for you will never fade. My desire for you will only grow.

And the life we share together will make every day worth living, because..."
Charlotte placed her fingers against his lips preventing him from finishing his declaration. Scowling as she took a step back from him, he concentrated on the loving expression on her face, instead of wondering why she stopped him.

Charlotte brought her finger's that were against his mouth to her lips and kissed them. He watched intently as she drug them down her chin to her chest. His heart was racing as her fingers traveled down between her breasts, across her stomach and stopped when they reached the inside of her hip.

Auggie glanced at her face just long enough to see her pull her lips into her mouth as she took a deep breath. Returning his focus to her fingers, resting against the inside of her hip, he watched her run a finger inside the band of her silk panties as she tugged one side of them down.

In an instant everything stopped. His heart, his breath, his being, everything escaped him as he went down on his knees in front of her. With a deep scowl Auggie clenched his back teeth together, almost unable to carry the weight of emotion inside him. Reaching his hand out, he wrapped it around her hip. As he brushed his thumb over the tiny letter A that was marked on the inside of her hip, Auggie gazed up at her. Kneeling in front of her, Auggie kept his eyes focused on Charlotte's as he placed a soft kiss against the inside of her hip. Slowly, he stood, taking her in his arms, swearing, "Because… You own me."

Chapter 25

Hours later, the afterglow of making love to her husband was far from wearing away. Swaying back and forth in Auggie's arms, while the wedding DJ played 'Fooled Around And Fell In Love' by Elvin Bishop, Charlotte reflected back on their moment.

In the midst of the slow steady rhythm, that satisfied her every desire, she could feel Auggie handing himself over to her. With each stroke, they grew closer. As his movements intensified, so did her feeling of ownership. When the moment came, Charlotte was more than complete, she was whole.

Brushing her lips against his, she wished the night was over and it was just the two of them.

"I love you."

Tightening his hold on her, he repeated, "I love you."

"Would it be wrong for us to sneak out of here?"

With a slight laugh, he replied, "After this song."

Smiling, she teased, "Because this is your theme song?"

"Our theme song." He clarified with a wink before asking, "You sure you're alright staying in the barn tonight?"

Curling the corner of her mouth into a smile, Charlotte replied, "Only if I get to wear the rubber boots."

Auggie appeared confused at first, then quickly took her by the hand and led her off of the wooden dance floor.

Making their way through the wedding guests, with polite nods and smiles, Charlotte noticed Braden standing by himself outside one of the party tents.

Tugging on Auggie's hand, she suggested, "We should see if he's okay."

Nodding, he agreed as they made their way over to him.

The closer they got the more it became clear that Braden was not okay.

"Hey, Braden." Charlotte greeted, causing him to look over at her and Auggie.

"Hey, Charlotte." He replied with a wide smile while reaching out to shake Auggie's hand.

Shaking his hand, Auggie asked, "Ya alright man?"

"Always." He assured, patting his brother on the back before turning and walking away.

As they continued to the truck, Charlotte glanced at Auggie and saw him shaking his head with a deep scowl.

By the time they made it to his truck, Charlotte couldn't keep quiet.

"He's not okay."

Opening the passenger door for her, Auggie scowled, saying, "I know."

"Do you need to talk to him?"

Shaking his head, he admitted, "I'm thinkin' I should listen instead."

"It's alright if you want to talk to him now."

Wrapping his arms around her waist, he kissed her before saying, "It can wait."

"You sure?"

Pulling her closer, Auggie shared, "Right now, there's a pair of rubber boots callin' me, and they've got your name on 'em, Mrs. Caffrey."

"Is that so, Mr. Caffrey?" She questioned with a laugh.

"Ya damn right." He confirmed, tossing her into the passenger seat of his truck.

The End

Acknowledgments

Always, Family First! I have the best one in the world!

Thank you to my readers! Without y'all my characters would never see the light of day.

All the INDIE blogger/reviewer/supporters out there, I appreciate everything that you do to keep writers writing.

Lucii my love ♥ this one would not have happened without you!

A very special 'thank you' to my beta readers Susanne Lancello, Nicole Griffin, Kasey Fitzgerald, Katelynn Luna, Paula Genereau. I am honored to have each of you in my corner, loving my characters.

To my Street Team, who spend countless hours, supporting and promoting so I can write, YOU LADIES ARE MY HEART!

Playlist

Music has a way of inspiring the smallest ideas. It allows me to create an entire scene or chapter from just the right song. For me, music is one of the most important creative tools there is.

There were only two songs I listened to while working on C&A. 'Crazy Love' by Brian McKnight and 'Fooled Around and Fell in Love' by Elvin Bishop.

About the Author

M. Sembera was born in Baton Rouge, Louisiana and now lives in Brazoria, Texas with her husband, three kids, three dogs and two cats. After writing her first short story when she was in high school, M. instantly fell in love with writing. However, life sometimes gets in the way of aspirations and it wasn't until years later, when her life calmed down, M. was able to start writing again.

'For me, each new book I write or character I create feels like the first time and I find myself falling in love with writing all over again'

Past works include Enduring Everything, Charlotte, One Penny, and 'The Rennillia Series'.

www.BrokenBirdMedia.com

Work in Progress

Marked Heart
Fall 2015

www.ingramcontent.com/pod-product-compliance
Lightning Source LLC
Chambersburg PA
CBHW060435130626
46555CB00005B/2372